To:

_____

From:

_____

A CHRISTMAS BELL
for Anya

As Narrated by Claire Bloom
with the Mormon Tabernacle Choir

Written by Chris & Evie Stewart
Illustrated by Ben Sowards

SHADOW
MOUNTAIN®

MORMON
TABERNACLE
CHOIR®

Text © 2006 Chris Stewart and Evie Stewart
Illustrations © 2006 Ben Sowards

The Artist wishes to thank Mark Galperin of Blagovest Bells.

Visit us at shadowmountain.com

Library of Congress Cataloging-in-Publication Data
Stewart, Chris, 1960–
A Christmas bell for Anya / Chris Stewart and Evie Stewart ;
illustrated by Ben Sowards.
p. cm.
ISBN-10 1-59038-636-1 (alk. paper)
ISBN-13 978-1-59038-636-1 (alk. paper)
1. Christmas stories. 2. Russia—Fiction. I. Stewart, Evie II. Sowards, Ben.
III. Title.
PS3569.T4593C48 2006
813'.54—dc22   2006012814

Printed in Mexico
R. R. Donnelley and Sons, Reynosa, Mexico

10   9   8   7   6   5   4   3   2   1

To our children—
Sean, Dane, Lance, Kayla,
Brice, and Megan
—C. & E.S.

For my son, Jared
—B.S.

I f it is true that you appreciate most what you don't often have, then the people of

Listbolski, Russia, loved the warmth of the spring more than any other people on earth.

The Siberian winters were long, cold, bitter, and mercilessly dark. Week after week, the

snow would gather, until the Sayan Mountains around the village were an unending

blanket of smooth, white snow. The skies were almost always gray and lifeless, though

there were occasional days when the north wind would blow, clearing the air to an

eye-piercing blue.

The people of Listbolski lived simple lives. They didn't have a lot—a little wood for their fires, a little oil for their lamps. They didn't expect very much, yet they always had hope. And they had their families. And that seemed to be enough.

During the winter of 1917, the entire state of Russia had fallen into dark and
tumultuous times, as the reign of the Czars came to a terrible, violent end. What was to
replace it, the people of Listbolski didn't know, but rumors of marauding soldiers and war
had reached the village, leaving the villagers with dark concerns to fill the long nights.

Anya was eight years old when she became aware of the violent upheaval around her. Though she was young, she was particularly sensitive for her age, and she knew, sometimes even more than the others, that a great danger was near.

Through the long winter, she and her father would often sit next to their fire, talking

and listening to the cold wind blow outside. On these evenings, her father would sometimes

gaze at her and think. *So much like her mother. The same bright smile. The same dark eyes.*

He loved Anya more than anything he had left in this world.

Though Listbolski was but a small village, there was one thing it was famous for. You see, the village artisans created the finest Christmas bells in the world, the red brass producing the clearest sound one could hear. Because of this, Listbolski had a Christmas tradition that went back many generations. Each year, the newest baby boy from the village

was selected to represent the Christ child. On Christmas morning, he would be wrapped in

a blanket and laid in a manger in the town square. Twelve village girls, dressed as angels,

were selected to stand around the child, each of them sounding her bell to ring in

Christmas morn.

The year she turned eight, Anya was selected to be one of the angels standing beside

the Christ child. Out of all the children in the village, she was one of the few!

As Christmas approached, she lay awake, the blankets pulled completely over the top of her head, dreaming of the morning when she would ring her own bell.

For weeks her father labored feverishly, knowing the final product had to be his very best work. Finally, just three days before Christmas, he brought Anya's bell home.

With his excited daughter on his knee, he laid his tools on the table and, working

together, they etched these words into the smooth metal on the inside of the bell:

"For My Angel to Ring on Christmas Morn."

Anya watched, her eyes blazing, as her father etched the words. Then she picked

up the bell and held it as if it were made of pure gold.

Turning to her father, she put her slender arms around his neck. "I really want to ring

my bell Christmas morning," she said.

He nodded at her happily. "I know that you do."

"I love you, Father," she whispered as she clutched her bell.

That night they came. Half an army, half a mob, they tore through the village with a dark and hateful fury.

They set fires. They killed and they randomly destroyed. Then they rode away on their

horses, their flaming torches illuminating the night.

orning found Anya's father weeping over his child. He had wrapped her in a blanket and held her until her tiny body was cold. As the glow of the fire faded, he looked up and cried, "God, why my daughter? Why my child?!"

For two days he sat alone on his wooden chair. He didn't eat. He didn't sleep. He

hardly had the will to breathe.

Afraid of the anger and the pain that consumed him, his soul cried out in anguish and loneliness. Enveloped by such darkness and without any strength, he did the only thing he could. Moving beneath his pain toward the small light still buried within him, he whispered, "Thank you, God, for letting me be Anya's father for eight years.

Thank you for the afternoon she helped me etch the words on her bell." For a moment, his simple acceptance seemed to soften his grief.

The night passed, and the day finally came, finding him still alone.

He listened to the village outside his home coming to life; the sound of people, some of them singing, then children's voices. Hard as their lot had become, the villagers knew they had to go on with their lives.

He forced himself to his feet and turned toward his cottage door. Numb and silent, he

slowly walked to the village square. Gathering with the others, he knelt at the manger of

the Christ child, then lifted his eyes to the angels, each of them holding a bell. And as the

young girls began their ringing, he listened to the pealing of the bells and knew that the

message of Christmas was real.

The sound of the bells slowly faded, and the silence of the mountains returned. The

villagers tarried, reluctant to break the spirit of that Christmas morning; but the cold

eventually drove them back to their homes, the sounds of their footsteps muffled by the

newly fallen snow, leaving Anya's father alone at the manger.

At last, he turned and started walking away from the square when, lifting his eyes to the morning light, he suddenly stopped.

He didn't see her, but he knew; somehow he knew that Anya was near.

Then he felt her whisper the message she wanted him to hear. "He was born, Father, so

that I might live. I'm still living, Father, and I'll be waiting for you."

He fell to his knees in the snow, overcome with relief and gratitude. A sudden warmth seemed to fill him as her words touched his heart. "Ring the bell for me, Father. Ring it every Christmas morn. He was born and He lives now. So think of Him. Think of me. And ring our bell every Christmas morn."